Ronald`s Dumb Computer

Ronald`s Dumb Computer

ROBERT W. BLY

Illustrated by Hodges Soileau

Miles Standish Press

Published by
Miles Standish Press, Inc.
37 West Avenue
Wayne, Pennsylvania 19087

Dell ® TM 681510, Dell Publishing Co., Inc.
ISBN: 0-440-07486-X

Printed in the United States of America
First Printing—September 1983

Dedication

For the Sprechers—Tom, Pat, and Andy

Acknowledgments

I'd like to thank my editors, Eric Marks, for suggesting the story line of *Ronald's Dumb Computer,* and Ed Claflin, for helping me shape my original manuscript into publishable form; my parents, sister, and wife, for their support and encouragement; and Gary Blake, for getting me started in this business. Also, thanks go to Karl Capek, whose play *R.U.R.* inspired the concept of this book.

Foreword: A Note to Teachers and Other Adults

This book is a fantasy—the story of two teenagers and the robot they found in the town dump.

But the story teaches as it entertains. It's written to show young adults how computers work and how computer programmers use logic to get their machines to perform.

All robots—real and imaginary—are simply computers that walk, talk and resemble human beings. As the teenagers in *Ronald's Dumb Computer* attempt to get the robot to do their bidding, they're forced to learn the ways of computer logic and language. It's the only language a robot—or a computer—understands. And so, when they want Ronald's robot to dust their rooms, they have to write a robot program to get him to do it. If they make a mistake along the way, readers will know it—and learn what is wrong and how to fix it.

This isn't a text on computer programming; no technical terms are used here. But in following the adventures of a sister and brother and their friendly robot, readers will learn—in a fun, easy way—what computers are, how they work, and how we must talk to them properly to get them to do our work.

The lot in back of the Ridgeville Industrial Park was not an official town dump, but it was filled with garbage anyway—broken glass, empty barrels, cables and rusting piles of machine parts. Many of the companies in the Park had dumped unwanted, unused materials and parts on the land behind their plants. This was cheaper than paying someone to haul the equipment off to the official town dump. And no one seemed to mind. Especially Ronald Smith.

Ronald loved to pick through the piles of discarded machinery and come up with hidden treasures. One time he found some radio tubes and transistors. On another visit he discovered the insides of a television set, bundles of colored wire, a typewriter keyboard, and a roll of brown magnetic tape. And finally he uncovered a three-ring notebook filled with computer print-outs. Although he didn't understand the strange-looking code it contained, he kept the binder on a shelf in his room.

Ronald was kind of disappointed in the dump. Most of the things he found didn't work and couldn't be used for anything. But still, Ronald kept his junkyard treasures on his shelves or in his desk. He knew that when he grew up he would be a chemist, an electrician or a computer programmer. Maybe he'd even design video games like Pac-Man, Donkey Kong or Space Invaders.

Maybe he'd do all of these things. He didn't know yet. But he figured all his junkyard stuff would come in handy one day.

His sister, Jenny, thought Ronald was crazy to keep all that junk around. Jenny loved plants, flowers, poems, dancing, pretend-games, painting, and stories about romantic, faraway places. When she grew up, she'd be a famous ballerina or an artist. Or both.

Frankly, Ronald thought dancing and flowers were boring. And Jenny couldn't have cared less about Ronald's junk collection. Still, they were friends when they weren't fighting. And they did a lot of things together—except go to the junkyard. "I don't want a broken TV set or cracked radio tubes," Jenny explained. "Besides, it's too messy." But Ronald was persistent—he thought they'd have fun exploring together, and four hands were better than two. He asked Jenny to come with him just about every Saturday.

Finally, one grey weekend morning, when there was nothing good on television and she didn't feel like doing anything else, she gave in.

Much later, she was glad she had.

They had just come through the gate of the junkyard. Ronald was looking over some old machinery piled near the back of the fence when suddenly he called out: "Jen, come here—quick!"

"What is it?"

"It's . . . it's a *man*."

Jenny walked over to where Ronald knelt by a scrap heap. He was hunched over a body. And it *was* a man . . . a metal man.

The robot was made of silvery, burnished metal from head to toe, and his surface was covered with rust. Two arms and two legs extended from his thick torso, connected by joints that looked like the middle part of an accordion. There were three separate hinged doors covering three compartments on his chest and abdomen, and the head, looking something like an upside-down bucket, had empty electrical sockets where the ears, eyes and mouth should have been. Below the opening for a mouth was an opening about

the size of a mail slot. Atop the head sat a dome full of colored Christmas lights. All the bulbs were dark.

Ronald reached for the top door on the robot's chest. Slowly, the rusted hinges gave way as he pulled it open.

Inside the door was a row of switches. They all were in the "down" position. There was writing underneath the switches, but the metal was rusted and Ronald couldn't read it.

"I'm going to flip a switch and see what happens," said Ronald.

"Don't!" cried Jenny. "You don't know what the switches are for. Maybe one is a self-destruct button. The robot might explode!"

"That's ridiculous," snorted Ronald. "They don't build machines with self-destruct buttons. I'm going to press a switch and see what happens."

Ronald flipped the switch.

Instantly, the lights in the dome atop the robot's head came on, and the dome rose up about five inches on its shaft. Humming, whirring and clicking noises came from the robot's chest and head. Both its arms stiffened. The legs kicked, as if the robot were stretching after a long nap. One arm hit Jenny on the shin. She toppled backward and landed in a sitting position, right on top of an old army footlocker. The locker was made of the same metal as the robot.

"Are you okay, Jen?" Ronald asked. She was staring at the locker.

"Ronny, look at this!" She pointed to words written on the box: Robot Spare Parts Kit.

Ronald opened the locker. Inside, parts were fitted neatly into compartments. And each compartment had a clear label:

Problem-viewer	Spare Brains (memory only)—(2)
Voice	Writing
Sight	Translator
Hearing	Instruction Paper
Shelves	Instruction Manual

Ronald paused a moment. A smile crossed his face and he reached into the compartment for the part labeled "Voice."

"This is going to be easy, Jen," he proclaimed. "After all, this guy is just a robot—and a robot is nothing more than a computer with legs and arms. And I know how to put a computer together!"

"Well, how?" asked Jenny.

"It's simple," replied Ronald. "Every computer has four simple parts: a brain, a memory, a part that lets you talk to the computer, and a part that lets the computer talk to you. This box must have all the parts for the robot! And I'm going to attach them!"

Ronald stood back. Now the robot had ears and a mouth where they should be. The spare brain fit neatly into a socket on the back of the robot's head. It was time to see whether the robot would work as Ronald had predicted.

"Hello," Ronald said.

Nothing.

"Hello?"

Nothing.

"Maybe he doesn't speak English," Jenny suggested a bit sarcastically. "Maybe he's a Spanish robot."

"Shut up, Jen," warned Ronald.

Just then they heard a police car siren from the highway beyond the dump. The robot heard it, too! He turned his head toward the sound and began emitting quick tones—high-pitched bleeps alternating with low-pitched blips. It sounded like someone playing two notes on an electric organ.

"He's talking!" shouted Ronald. "That's how he talks. In bleeps."

"Great," said Jenny. "But there's just one problem. *We* don't talk in blips or bleeps; we talk in English."

"So what!" said Ronald, not about to give up. "We'll just have to learn his language, or teach him ours. Or maybe," he said, "the answer's sitting in his spare parts case."

Just as Ronald suggested, the spare parts case contained a translator device that translated the robot's blips and bleeps into human language. The translator fit neatly into the interior of the robot's right ear. Ronald also installed the sight device so the robot could see where it was going.

"Now he's ready to go," Ronald announced.

"Wait a minute," said Jenny. "What's this?" She pointed to the compartment in the box labeled "Instruction Paper." It contained a stack of brown paper and a black felt-tip pen.

Ronald examined the paper. Then he looked at the mail-slot opening on the robot's face.

"I think we have a choice," he said. "It looks like we can talk to the robot in two different ways. We can write down what we want him to do on this special paper. Or we can speak with him directly. Let's start by writing instructions. That way, we'll be able to keep notes on what he understands and what he doesn't."

"There isn't much paper in the box," Jenny pointed out.

Ronald frowned. "I know," he said. "We'll just have to command him aloud after we run out."

Ronald used the marker to write the words "STAND UP" on the special brown paper. He placed the paper in the robot's mouth slot; the paper was pulled from Ronald's grasp and sucked into the slot. Relays clicked. Gears turned. Blips were emitted from the mouthpiece. And then . . .

The robot stood up!

"It works!" cried Ronald. "He'll do whatever we tell him. Watch!" Ronald picked up a stick, threw it as far as he could, then wrote "RETREIVE THE STICK" on the paper. As before, the robot accepted the sheet. But instead of fetching the stick, the robot's lights began blinking rapidly, a buzzer sounded, and the paper came spewing out of the slot. The robot had added words to the page. Now it read:

RETREIVE THE STICK

ERROR ERROR ERROR

"I don't get it," said Ronald, puzzled. "What did I do wrong?"

"Let me see," said Jenny. She studied the page. "Here it is—you misspelled the word 'retrieve.' It should be R, E, T, R, *I*, *E*, V, E—not *E*, *I*, V, E."

"Ridiculous," snorted Ronald. "I *meant* 'retrieve.' What difference does spelling make?"

"Don't take my word. Try again. But spell it the right way and see what happens."

"Or, I could check the parts kit," Ronald suggested. "I remember seeing an instruction manual. Maybe the instructions will help us control the robot better."

Ronald took the package labeled "Instruction Manual" from the spare parts locker. Only it wasn't a booklet. The instruction manual was a thin metal tablet with a silvery screen covering one flat surface. As soon as Ronald unwrapped it, words formed on the screen like magic:

> THIS MANUAL IS PROVIDED TO HELP YOU TALK WITH AND INSTRUCT YOUR "UNIVERSAL ROBOT #334-J2-N/PAT-1." WHEN YOU THINK OF A QUESTION, YOUR ANSWER WILL APPEAR ON THE TABLET'S SCREEN. THIS MANUAL COVERS ONLY THE GENERAL RULES OF OPERATION. NATURALLY, YOU WILL HAVE TO USE YOUR OWN KNOWLEDGE OF ROBOT PROGRAMMING TO WRITE ANY SPECIAL INSTRUCTIONS FOR THE UNIVERSAL ROBOT TO FOLLOW.

"It appears I am the proud owner of a Universal Robot, whatever *that* is," said Ronald. "I think I'll name him R.U.R.—short for Ronald's Universal Robot."

I wonder, Ronald thought while concentrating on the tablet, *do spelling errors confuse the robot*?

The tablet answered:

> YOUR UNIVERSAL ROBOT OPERATES ON STRICT RULES OF LOGIC. ALL INSTRUCTIONS MUST BE PRECISE. THE ROBOT CAN ACCEPT ONLY CORRECT INSTRUCTIONS—FREE FROM ERRORS IN SPELLING, PUNCTUATION AND GRAMMAR. HE CANNOT UNDERSTAND INSTRUCTIONS THAT ARE IN ERROR BECAUSE HE CANNOT THINK AS HUMANS DO. THE ROBOT CAN DO ONLY WHAT YOU TELL HIM TO DO.

"I was right," smirked Jenny when she saw the tablet's print-out. "Now, let's try it *my* way."

Jenny took the paper, wrote "RETRIEVE THE STICK," and fed it into RUR. Immediately the robot set off to fetch the stick Ronald had thrown.

Then Ronald and Jenny made a deal. Ronald would write programs to tell the robot what to do. Jenny would check them for spelling and grammar.

When RUR returned with the stick Jenny realized how late it was—almost time for supper.

They hid RUR in the junk pile and went home. Later they returned and, in the darkness, put an old blanket over the robot. The robot followed them home, through the back door, and upstairs into Ronald's room. Their parents, busy reading or watching TV, didn't hear a thing.

"But what can we do with him?" complained Jenny when they uncovered RUR. "If he takes a walk while Mom and Dad are home, they'll hear his big feet clumping around the room."

Ronald was writing instructions. "RUR's going to be too busy for a while to play with us," he said.

"Why?"

Ronald winked at her. "Because I'm writing instructions to tell him how to do our homework."

"Let's start him off with simple addition," Ronald suggested. He fed in a paper with the instructions: "2+2."

Nothing happened.

"Maybe he needs some oil," Ronald said. "Better check the instruction manual and see what's wrong."

"Wait," said Jenny. "Remember what it said the last time about good grammar? Well, in math, 2+2 isn't good grammar because it's not a complete sentence."

Ronald was puzzled. "Why not?"

Jenny explained. "The statement '2+2' doesn't tell the robot to do anything."

Ronald nodded. RUR said nothing.

"So in math," Jenny continued, "2+2 isn't really complete. We have to say more. Like so." She wrote "X=2+2" on the paper and then fed it to RUR. They heard the clicking of gears as RUR computed the value of X. But there was still no answer from the robot.

"Wait a second," said Ronald. "We've been acting like dummies. We've got to tell RUR everything we want him to do—and in the right order, too." Ronald grabbed a fresh piece of brown paper and wrote down the following steps:

```
1 LET X=2+2
2 PRINT X
3 END
```

RUR swallowed the slip of paper. In an instant it popped out with the answer: 4.

"That's neat," said Jenny. "I wonder how he works?"

"I don't know," replied Ronald.

The next day Ronald and Jenny went to get RUR's parts kit from the dump. The locker was just where they'd left it the last time. Together they carried the locker home.

Ronald removed the problem-viewer from the box. It was a device that looked like a pair of binoculars. Then he opened one of the doors on RUR's chest and peered into the robot's inner workings with the problem-viewer. Then he suggested that Jenny take a look. Inside RUR's chest, she saw a bunch of tiny mailboxes.

Ronald explained what they meant. "According to the robot's instruction manual, this is RUR's memory—the part of his electronic brain that lets him store our instructions. Each place in memory is like a post office box. Either it has mail in it or it doesn't. In RUR's brain, each box can hold only one piece of mail, and each piece of mail is really a piece of information.

"Each mailbox is labeled with a letter of the alphabet. Take a look at the post office box marked 'X.' What's in it?"

"The number 4," reported Jenny.

"That's right," said Ronald, pleased. "Remember our computer program? The first line of the program told RUR to let the value of X equal 2 plus 2. When RUR read that instruction, he computed

16

the value of 2 plus 2 and got 4. Then he stored it in the mailbox labeled 'X.'"

Ronald continued. "Step 2—PRINT X—told RUR to print out any information in the X box . . . which, because of our instructions, was the number 4. Step 3, END, told RUR that he was finished carrying out our instructions."

"It's like baking cookies," said Jenny. "Just take the basic ingredients, follow the instructions from the cookbook, and you get a batch of cookies. Only, in the kitchen, Mom or Dad helps me sometimes. But even so, I don't think they'd know what to do with old RUR here."

"Or it's like building a model. All the instructions have to be done in the right order or else RUR won't come up with the right answer."

"Now that we know what makes him tick, let's get on with our math homework," Jenny told Ronald.

"Let's try multiplication," said Ronald. "We'll multiply 6,000,000,000 by 3,500,000,000." He fed the program into RUR. An instant later came the print-out:

ERROR ERROR OVERFLOW OVERFLOW

"What's wrong *now*?" asked Jenny impatiently. Frankly, she was beginning to get annoyed with RUR. She thought it would be easier to do homework the regular way, and she told Ronald so.

"Jenny, you're right. We can add 2 plus 2 faster than it takes to program RUR to do it," Ronald replied. "But RUR has a computer for a brain. Once we tell him how to do something, he can do it over and over again without getting tired or bored. And I'd guess that he can do hundreds, maybe thousands of calculations every second. If you had six pages of math problems to do, all the same kind, RUR could handle the whole assignment in just a few seconds—once we got the instructions running properly, that is."

Jenny frowned. "But he can't even multiply 6 billion by 3½ billion. What's an 'overflow'? Is his brain overflowing?"

"That must be it!" exclaimed Ronald. "Let's use the problem-viewer to take a look and find out."

They peered through those strange binoculars and this time they were able to see RUR's brain. It looked like a cup full of numbers, only the numbers were too big to fit into the cup. Extra numbers sloshed over the rim and spilled out of the brain. The problem was clear: there was a limit to the size of the numbers RUR could handle. A billion seemed to be about the biggest number that could fit into his brain. Bigger numbers would simply spill out.

"RUR can't solve the problem because he can't multiply big numbers," decided Ronald.

"Well, then let's give him small numbers," Jenny replied.

"What do you mean?" Ronald asked.

"If RUR's limited brain-power can't handle big numbers," she explained, "we'll just make the numbers smaller by dividing them by a billion. Instead of telling RUR to multiply 6 billion and 3½ billion, we'll just have him multiply 6 times 3½. And when RUR gives us the answer to 6 times 3½, we'll just multiply that by a billion times a billion. That will give us the answer to the original problem."

Sure enough, when RUR was given the new problem, he came up with the answer, 21, in an instant. It was a simple matter for Jenny to add on eighteen zeros and get the answer of 21,000,000,000,000,000,000.

RUR sat in the corner of Ronald's room, unmoving. Once programmed, it had taken RUR only a minute to complete the week's math homework. But Jenny had other things she wanted him to do.

"How about chores?" she asked Ronald. "He's not just a pocket calculator; he has arms and legs and hands and feet. Why not put him to work? He could clean our rooms and do our chores!"

"I suppose," said Ronald absently, as he stared at RUR. Poor robot. When they'd found RUR, they had thought of him as a playmate. But once they'd discovered how obedient he was, it was hard not to use this uncomplaining metal man to do their homework. Ronald knew that computers were built to do all kinds of tasks faster than people could. But he felt guilty turning RUR into a slave—maybe because RUR was one computer that looked human. Or semi-human, anyway.

"Well," urged Jenny impatiently. "Can you get him to clean our rooms?"

"You understand how he works," Ronald replied. "Why don't *you* try it?"

"Okay," agreed Jenny. She took a piece of instruction paper and wrote "CLEAN UP THIS ROOM" on it. Then she fed it to RUR.

Ronald and Jenny watched with fascination as RUR's left hand retracted into the arm. A second later, it came out. Only it wasn't a hand, but some kind of round disk that looked like a scouring pad. RUR made a clicking noise and the disk began to rotate at fantastic speed. Without warning, RUR pushed it against the wall. Chips went flying as the wire pad chewed away the plaster!

"Stop!" cried Ronald.

RUR stopped.

"What do you think you're doing?" Jenny demanded of the robot. RUR did not reply.

"It's not his fault," Ronald defended RUR. "Whoever made RUR must have programmed him to do that when he's instructed to 'CLEAN.' Maybe he was used on an automobile assembly line to buff and polish car bodies.

"Anyway, if we want him to clean your room, we're going to have to write a specific program to show him how," finished Ronald.

Ronald realized that trying to write a program to do something as complex as cleaning a room isn't as simple as it sounds. RUR, he knew, was capable of following step-by-step instructions. And those instructions had to be precise. If they were vague, or out of order, the robot might wreck the room. Or not get any work done at all.

"Jen," he said, "this program is too big to tackle all at once. Let's break the job of cleaning the room into a bunch of separate tasks. Then we can write a program to handle each one. Why don't you make a list of everything we have to do when we clean our rooms."

Here is what Jenny wrote on the paper:

DUSTING
VACUUMING
PICKING UP CLOTHES
PUTTING AWAY CLOTHES
PICKING UP TOYS
PUTTING AWAY TOYS
MAKING THE BED

Ronald added two items to Jenny's list:

EMPTYING THE WASTE BASKET
WASHING THE WINDOWS

"These are the jobs RUR has to do when he cleans the room," said Ronald. "Pick one and he can get started."

Jenny wrote "DUST" on a slip of RUR's special brown instruction paper.

"Let's have him dust first and see how he does," said Jenny. "Then we can program the other jobs."

"Sounds good to me," said Ronald. "While he's dusting, we can see what's on TV." Jenny and Ronald fed the slip of paper with the instruction "DUST" to RUR and went downstairs to watch TV in the den.

They watched *Godzilla vs. Megalon*, a science fiction movie about a Japanese scientist who invents a robot he can command with a remote-control device. But when a monster threatens to destroy Earth, the robot takes on a will of its own and comes to Earth's rescue; and the robot can no longer be controlled by the scientist's commands. The movie made Ronald wonder—and

worry—whether RUR could begin to make up his own mind about things. If that happened, would the robot still do homework and chores for Ronald and his sister? Or would he go back where he came from?

After the show was over, Ronald and Jenny went upstairs to check RUR's progress. But what they got was a real shock!

Every piece of furniture in the room was covered with a thick coat of dust. And in the middle of the room stood RUR—spraying a stream of dust onto the floor from an opening in his chest.

"RUR, stop!" Ronald shouted.

Instantly, the dust spraying stopped. RUR stood motionless, waiting for the next instruction.

Ronald examined the dust and saw that it was sawdust—wood shavings. He knew that in some machine shops, the workers spread sawdust on the floor so they wouldn't slip on spilled oil. Now he suspected that RUR had been built to work in an industrial plant. Except that no industrial robot he'd ever seen in a magazine or on television was nearly as advanced as RUR. No robot on *Earth*, that is. . . .

"Dummy!" Jenny scolded RUR. "We told you to take dust *off* the furniture, not put dust *on* the furniture." She kicked his shin and then howled in pain as she stubbed her toe on the metal. RUR did not move or speak.

"Calm down, Jen," said Ronald. "RUR's not the dummy—*I* am, for thinking that RUR would be able to read our minds. How could he know exactly what we meant when we said 'DUST'?"

"I'm afraid we'll have to write a detailed, step-by-step program on dusting," Ronald continued. Ronald wrote down the steps of the program:

TAKE OBJECTS OFF THE FURNITURE
DUST OFF THE FURNITURE WITH A CLOTH
PUT OBJECTS BACK ON THE FURNITURE
DUST OFF THE NEXT PIECE OF FURNITURE

"Do you think that should do it?" he asked Jenny.

Jenny took a look at the list and added more instructions:

1 GET A DUST CLOTH
2 WALK OVER TO A PIECE OF FURNITURE
3 TAKE OBJECTS OFF THE FURNITURE
4 DUST OFF THE FURNITURE
5 PUT OBJECTS BACK ON THE FURNITURE
6 GO TO THE NEXT PIECE OF FURNITURE AND REPEAT STEPS 1-5 FOR ALL THE PIECES OF FURNITURE IN THE ROOM

Ronald frowned as he studied the paper.

"There's nothing wrong with my program," Jenny said defensively. "You don't have to keep looking at it. Let's give it to RUR. It'll work, you'll see."

"Will it?" asked Ronald. "I see a few problems with it."

"For example?"

"For one thing, the instructions don't tell RUR to check whether the furniture even needs to be dusted. According to what we've written, RUR will dust every piece of furniture in the room whether it's dusty or not."

"You're right," agreed Jenny. "And there's another problem. Step 4 tells RUR to dust the furniture. But how does he know when to stop dusting? We've got to tell him to give it the 'white glove test,' or else he just might keep dusting forever!"

"But we're getting somewhere!" Ronald cried. "You know, it's helpful to check over RUR's program step-by-step before we give it to him. It lets us catch mistakes in the instructions, and RUR doesn't goof up everything because of a bad program."

"You're right," said Jenny. "From now on, we should go through all of RUR's programs this way. If it's a program for doing a chore, we'll check to see whether the steps make sense. And whether they're perfectly clear."

"And if it's a program to do math homework, I'll work through it to make sure the right answers come out," offered Ronald.

"Let's get on with the dusting," persisted Jenny. "What's the next step?"

"Here," said Ronald, pulling a large piece of drawing paper from a pad. "I think it might help to draw a picture of the steps we want RUR to take."

Ronald began to put his list of instructions in picture form. This is what he drew:

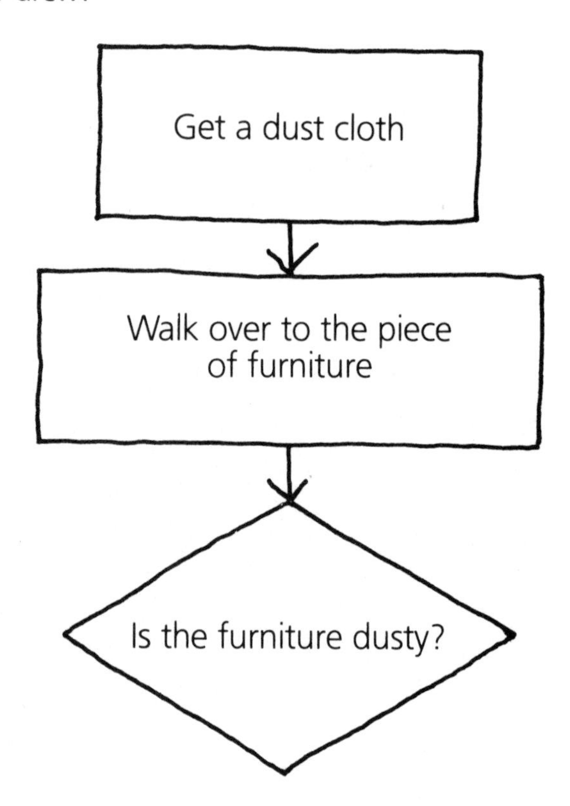

"The rectangles are the instructions," explained Ronald, "and the triangles mean RUR has to make a decision." He continued drawing:

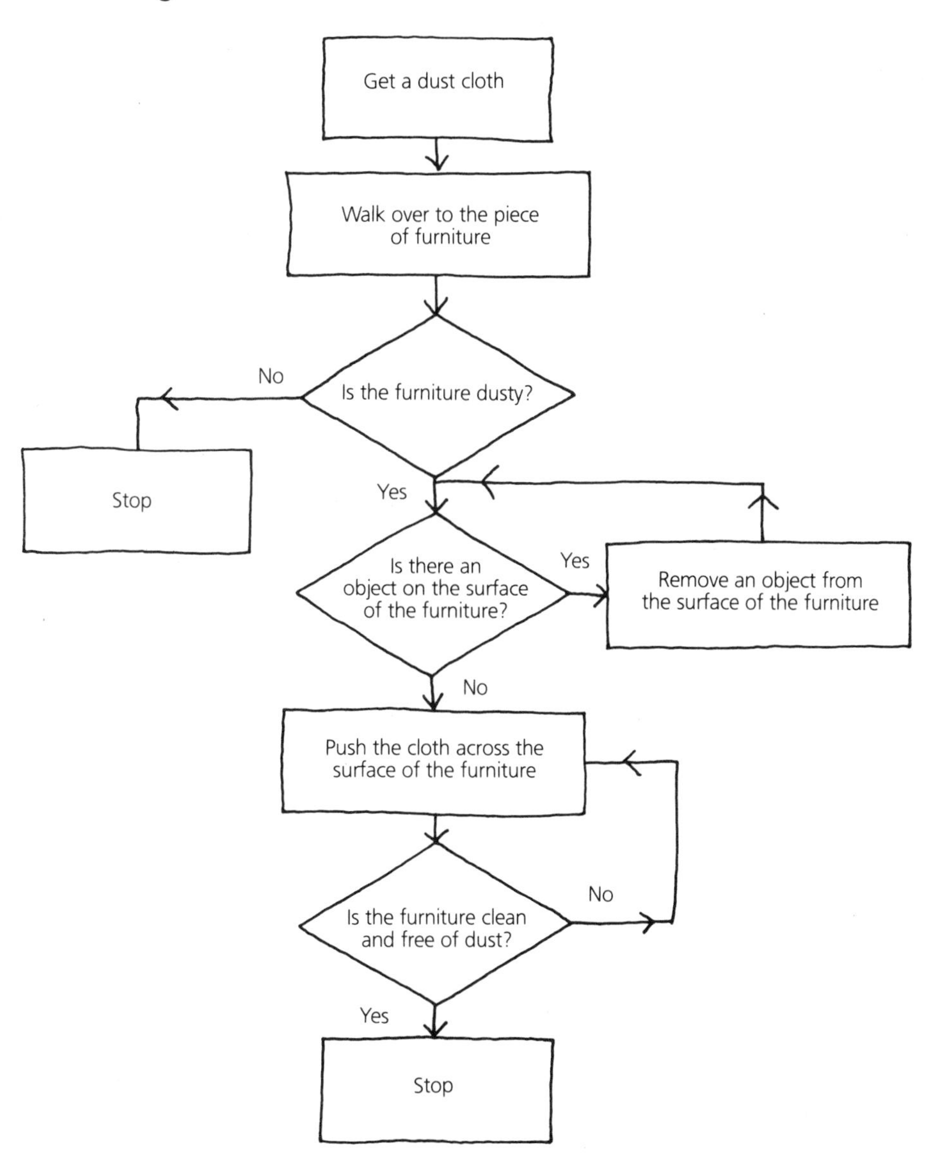

"There," said Ronald, "I'm done. First RUR gets the dust cloth and walks over to the furniture. He checks to see if it's dusty. If it's clean, then he doesn't dust, and the program ends—STOP. If it is dusty, he has to see if there's anything on top of the furniture. Otherwise, he might smash our things.

"Then," continued Ronald, "he dusts by pushing the cloth over the furniture. Every time he dusts, he checks to see if the furniture is clean. If it's not, he keeps dusting. When it's clean, he stops."

"Pretty good," admired Jenny. "But you've left an important step out."

"I have?" asked Ronald. "Where?"

"Simple," Jenny answered. "You forgot to tell RUR to put our things back on the furniture after he's dusted!"

"You're right," admitted Ronald. "But it's easy to fix. Watch." And he drew in the remaining step. Now the finished flow chart looked like this:

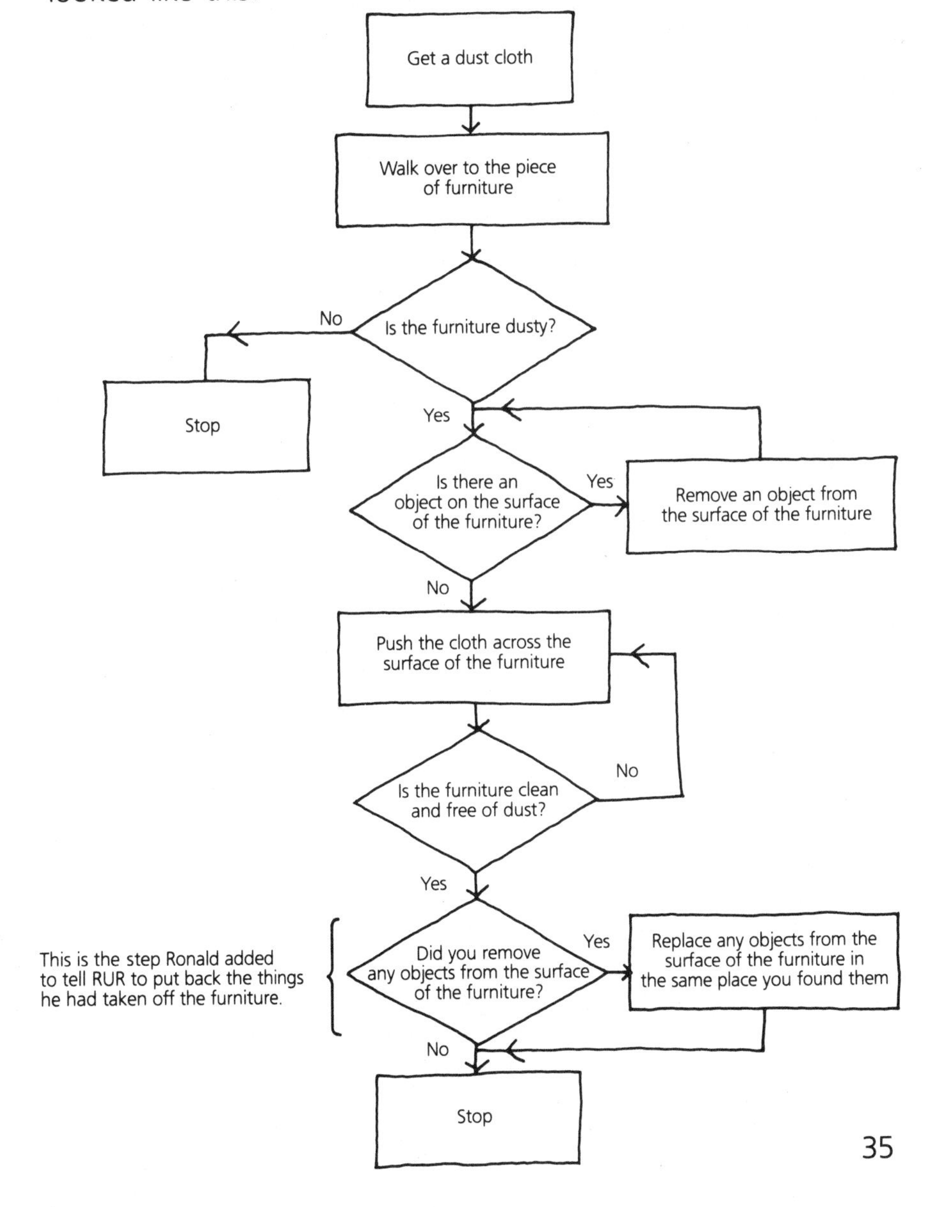

"Now, after RUR's finished dusting, he'll know to put things back before he stops working," said Ronald.

Both Ronald and Jenny studied the program for several minutes.

"Looks perfect," Jenny said. "Let's write it out on the instruction paper and see what happens."

Ronald wrote the program. As soon as RUR received it, his eyes and dome lit up. He stretched his metal arms in a robotlike yawn. Then he whisked a dust cloth off Ronald's desk and began to go to work.

"It's a success!" Jenny yelled. Both Ronald and Jenny watched with pride as the robot gently removed Ronald's chemistry set from his desk, one piece at a time. "Let's go downstairs and have some lunch," said Ronald. "I'm starved!"

They left RUR to his work. Two peanut butter and jelly sandwiches, three glasses of milk, and eight chocolate chip cookies later, they returned to check RUR's progress. Much to their dismay, they found him standing motionless over the desk! Instead of dusting the room, he had dusted only the desk and then, for some strange reason, had stopped working altogether.

"There's a problem with the program," Jenny announced, "and I know what it is.

"Take a look at the drawing. This isn't a program for dusting a roomful of furniture. It's a program for dusting a single piece of furniture! After RUR is finished dusting the first piece of furniture, the program tells him to stop. There's no reason for RUR to go on to another piece of furniture!"

"Then the program doesn't work," moaned Ronald. "Oh, well," he sighed, "I suppose we can still use it. We'll just have to check up on RUR every couple of minutes. If he's stopped dusting, we'll give him the program again and point him toward another piece of furniture. I guess that still beats doing the cleaning ourselves."

"There's a better way," replied Jenny. "We can fix the program."

Jenny drew a box around the program and labeled it a "mini-program." It looked like this:

Instructions for Dusting One Piece of Furniture: Mini-Program #1

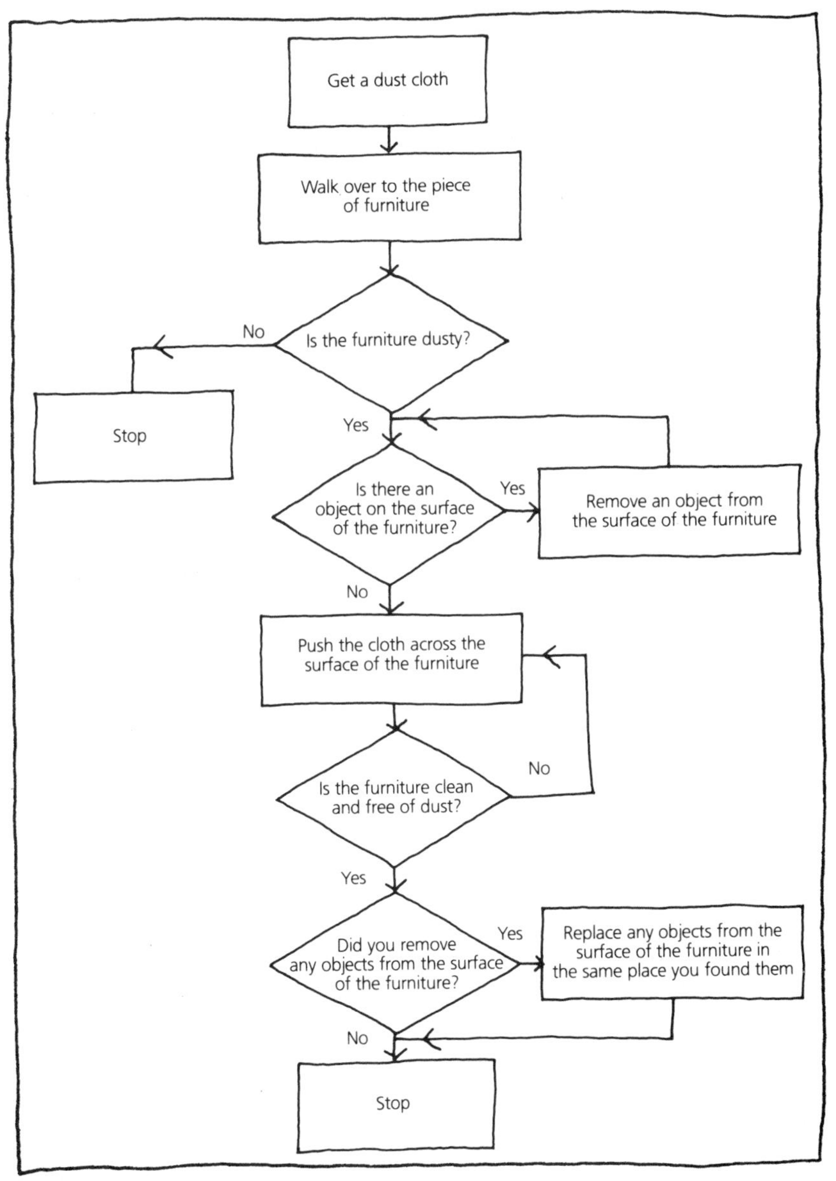

"Count me out," said Ronald. "It took us a long time to come up with this program and I'm not about to do it again."

"You don't have to redo the whole thing," Jenny insisted. "Just add a few steps."

"This I'd like to see," grumbled Ronald.

"Now," said Jenny, "we already have a mini-program to tell RUR to dust *one* piece of furniture. We can use it to write a bigger program that tells him to dust *every* piece of furniture in the room." She drew the new program on another piece of paper.

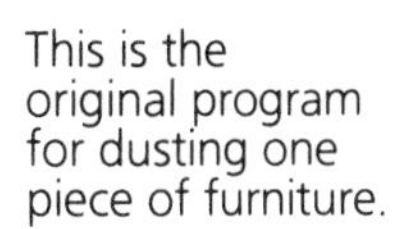

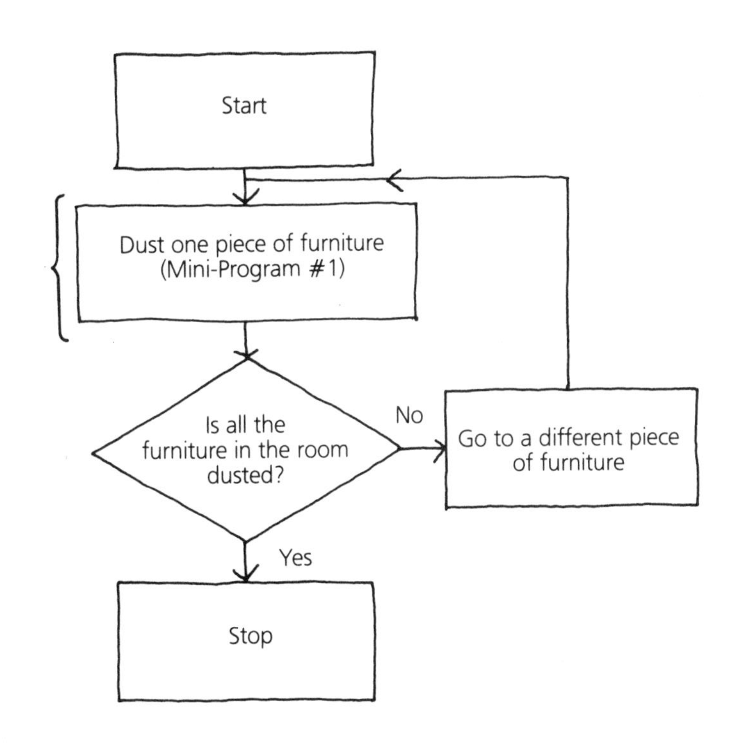

"Do you see how this works?" Jenny asked Ronald.

"I think so," he replied. "After RUR carries out the mini-program for dusting a single piece of furniture, the maxi-program asks if all the furniture in the room has been dusted. If it hasn't, he repeats the dusting routine on a new piece of furniture. And he keeps repeating it until all the furniture has been cleaned."

"That's the way it should work," said Jenny. She fed the new program through RUR's mouth slot.

The robot walked over to the dresser and began dusting.

And in just a few minutes RUR finished the whole room! What's more, he did it without complaining, without getting tired, and without asking for a drink of water!

Once Jenny and Ronald figured out how to program RUR to dust, getting him to do other chores was easy. They discovered that every chore can be divided into a series of steps. Sometimes a step had to be skipped, and other times RUR had to make a decision or compare two things to decide which step would be next. Programming RUR to vacuum was not too different from programming him to dust the room. And after that, it was easy programming him to pick up and put away clothes.

In time, they wrote programs to do everything on their original list of chores, including:

DUSTING
VACUUMING
PICKING UP CLOTHES
PUTTING AWAY CLOTHES
PICKING UP TOYS
PUTTING AWAY TOYS
MAKING THE BED
STRAIGHTENING OUT THE CLOSET
EMPTYING THE WASTE BASKET
WASHING THE WINDOWS

Each program was written on a separate sheet of brown paper and each sheet had a label. The dusting program was labeled "PROGRAM NUMBER ONE: DUSTING THE ROOM." The vacuuming program was labeled "PROGRAM NUMBER TWO: VACUUMING." And so on.

For a while, this collection of programs made life pretty easy for Ronald and Jenny. They kept the papers in a file in Ronald's top desk drawer. When Ronald or Jenny needed to do a chore, they'd simply take the program they wanted from the file, feed it to RUR, and he'd do the job, quick as a flash. Best of all, he never grumbled and always did the work perfectly.

But Ronald eventually became dissatisfied with this procedure. For one thing, he didn't want Jenny to go into his desk every time she wanted to run a program. For another, the program sheets were beginning to rip and tear from so much handling. And once, Ronald himself misplaced one of the sheets. He had to spend the better part of a Saturday rewriting the program from scratch. Clearly, there was a better way, and he suggested it to Jenny.

"RUR's got a lot of room inside him," Ronald pointed out. "I think a lot of that space is for his memory—where he keeps numbers and other information. Maybe he can store our programs there, too."

"But how would we find a program in there when we wanted to use it?" asked Jenny. "How would RUR even find the program? How could we tell him to remember where it is?"

"We've already put labels on our programs," Ronald pointed out. "The labels can tell us where in the memory the information is stored. By naming a label, RUR should be able to find a program in his memory."

Jenny reminded Ronald that they had written a number of other programs besides the housekeeping programs. They'd done programs to solve homework problems in algebra, physics, chemistry and basic arithmetic. Ronald had also written a few programs to play games with the computer. And Jenny had created a program to catalog her books and records.

"We need a system," declared Jenny. "A system for keeping track of—and finding—the programs we put into RUR's brain."

Ronald asked, "What are some ways people list things?"

Jenny thought a moment. "Catalogs," she said. "Catalogs and directories—like the phone book."

Ronald took notes. "Good. What else?"

"Let me see. . . . The library uses a card catalog to keep track of its books. Maybe we can make a library of programs."

"A library is good, but card catalogs are kind of hard to use. What's an easy way to list things you're going to want to look at and choose from?"

"How about a menu?" offered Jenny.

"That just might work out," said Ronald. "Why don't you write out the 'menus' for our robot programs?"

"Why not just put them all on the same menu and call it 'MENU OF ROBOT PROGRAMS'!"

"We could," Ronald answered slowly, "but remember, we have programs in a number of different categories. Some solve problems. Others instruct RUR to do chores. If you had a chain of restaurants, and each served a different type of food, you wouldn't have one single menu for all the restaurants. You'd have a menu for the American food, another for the Chinese and a third for the Italian."

All the time Ronald was lecturing, Jenny had been writing. "Here," she said, handing him a piece of paper, "here's how I'd arrange our menu of robot programs."

And here's what she had written:

ROBOT PROGRAM LIBRARY

SELECT FROM THE FOLLOWING MENUS OF PROGRAMS:

MENU A: HOUSEHOLD CHORES

MENU B: HOMEWORK

MENU C: SPECIAL PROGRAMS

MENU A: HOUSEHOLD CHORES

PROGRAM 1: DUSTING
PROGRAM 2: VACUUMING
PROGRAM 3: PICKING UP CLOTHES
PROGRAM 4: PUTTING AWAY CLOTHES
PROGRAM 5: PICKING UP TOYS
PROGRAM 6: PUTTING AWAY TOYS
PROGRAM 7: MAKING THE BED
PROGRAM 8: STRAIGHTENING OUT THE CLOSET
PROGRAM 9: EMPTYING THE WASTE BASKET
PROGRAM 10: WASHING THE WINDOWS

MENU B: HOMEWORK

PROGRAM 1: ALGEBRA
PROGRAM 2: ARITHMETIC
PROGRAM 3: CHEMISTRY
PROGRAM 4: PHYSICS

MENU C: SPECIAL PROGRAMS

PROGRAM 1: G-H-O-S-T GAME
PROGRAM 2: HANGMAN
PROGRAM 3: BATTLESHIP
PROGRAM 4: RONALD'S INCOME
PROGRAM 5: JENNY: BOOK CATALOG
PROGRAM 6: JENNY: RECORD CATALOG

Science

"Looks good," said Ronald, impressed by how quickly Jenny had completed the list. "That's how we'll do it."

Jenny smiled. She was enjoying learning to use the robot. This surprised her a bit, though, because she had always hated math and science. But teaching RUR wasn't boring like algebra or chemistry. It was fun.

Ronald was gathering the programs to feed them into RUR's memory. "When we want to use a program stored in memory, we'll ask RUR to 'LIST' the 'ROBOT PROGRAM LIBRARY,'" said Ronald. "Right now, the list will print out the three menus—A, B, and C. If we want to add more categories later, we can.

"Then, we'll select which menu we want to use and tell RUR to LIST MENU A, MENU B, or MENU C, depending on our choice. On this command, he'll print out all the programs listed under a particular menu. Then we just select the program we want by its number, and it'll be ready to go."

Ronald had collected all of the programs. He was ready to store them inside RUR's electronic memory. The only problem was, he wasn't quite sure how to go about it. . . .

Ronald spoke to the robot. "Okay, RUR, listen up. Are you listening?"

The robot nodded his head up and down.

"Good. Now, I'm going to feed you a whole bunch of programs at once. Don't *do* anything. Just keep the programs inside your brain—you know, whatever it is in your circuitry or mechanism that lets you remember things. Each program is labeled. In the future, when we give you the label's name, you'll find the program and run it. Okay?"

RUR nodded again.

Ronald fed the first program into RUR's input slot. Inside RUR, you could hear circuits buzzing and clicking, and the lights in his dome were switching on and off in rapid patterns. A small slip of brown paper came out of the slot, which Ronald took. The paper read, "INPUT COMPLETE: PROGRAM STORED IN MEMORY."

"Okay," said Ronald. "Here comes number two."

He fed another instruction paper into RUR's input slot. Again, circuits hummed. But this time, the lights in RUR's dome did not flash on and off. And when the slip of paper came out of RUR, it read, "ERROR ERROR MEMORY OVERLOAD."

"There goes that bright idea," said Ronald. "RUR must have a really tiny brain if he can store only a single program. I guess we'll just have to keep all the program sheets in the desk drawer."

But Jenny was not so easily daunted. "Before we give up," she said, "why don't we use the problem-viewer to see what's wrong?"

With the problem-viewer, the special set of magical binoculars that came with RUR's spare parts kit, Ronald and Jenny peered into RUR's interior workings. They saw a large wooden box. At the bottom of the box sat the first piece of instruction paper they'd fed into RUR. The second floated around the outside of the box. Ronald noticed lettering on the surface of the box. It read:

CONTENTS: SET OF PROGRAM INSTRUCTIONS
QUANTITY: ONE (1) SET PER CRATE COMPARTMENT

They were stymied. Obviously, thought Ronald, RUR's memory held programs like a carton held eggs. But RUR's carton could hold only one item at a time. Would RUR always be handicapped by the limits of his memory?

"Ron," said Jenny, "suppose you wanted to make an egg carton that could hold more than a dozen eggs. How would you do it?"

"I don't know. I guess I'd make one with extra egg compartments."

"And that's just what we're going to do with RUR!" replied his sister. She got up and retrieved the robot's spare parts kit. Quickly, she went through the kit to make sure it still contained a complete set of items:

Problem-viewer	Spare Brains (memory only)—(2)
Voice	Writing
Sight	Translator
Hearing	Instruction Paper
Shelves	Instruction Manual

They had already found uses for the problem-viewer, voice, sight, hearing, translator, instruction paper and instruction manual. Now, Jenny suspected she knew exactly what the shelves were designed for.

She removed the shelves from their compartments. They were thin sheets of metal, the same size as the programming paper. She fed them into RUR's input slot one by one. She heard a click from inside RUR's chest as each shelf fell into place. Looking through the problem-viewer, Jenny saw that the shelves were fitting into the memory box like the shelves on a bookcase.

Jenny had figured out that the number of items that can fit in a space depends not just on how big the space is, but on how it's used as well. Even the tallest bookcase can't hold many books unless it's divided with book shelves. And an egg carton has a separate compartment for holding each egg.

Jenny saw that RUR's memory was much the same. By using the shelves as partitions to divide the memory into many separate segments, she increased its capacity to hold programs, since each segment could hold one complete program sheet.

In no time, RUR's memory was divided into dozens of small, compact segments. Jenny fed in the program sheets and watched as each was deposited in a different location in memory. Now they could use the memory to call up any program they wanted.

By now, Ronald and Jenny had become fairly adept at writing robot programs. And they'd fixed RUR's memory so it could store dozens of them! But the next day, when Ronald and Jenny sat down to write a program to instruct RUR to wash the dishes, they made a shocking discovery: they were out of programming paper! The supply of special brown instruction paper they had found with RUR had been used up. And there was no way to get more of it.

Although there was no paper left, RUR could still hear and speak. So Ronald and Jenny decided to talk directly with the robot. After all, they had already stored most of their programs in RUR's memory. If they wanted him to dust, they could just ask him to carry out the dusting program, and he'd oblige them.

Ronald walked over to RUR and said, "RUR, today I want you to dust my furniture and make my bed."

"And I want you to clean *my* room, too," Jenny added.

RUR stood up. He took a step toward Ronald's bed, then stopped and turned in the other direction, toward Jenny's room. It seemed as if he couldn't decide where to go first. And sure enough, as he took a step back toward Ronald's bed, he froze in his tracks and spoke in his flat, mechanical voice: "WARNING . . . WARNING . . . CONFLICT . . . CONFLICT . . ." After that, he remained silent and didn't move.

"RUR, are you all right?" Jenny asked, approaching the immobile machine. She snapped her fingers. She tried tapping her knuckles against his silver metal skin. Nothing. He remained frozen.

"Ronald, do you know what's wrong with RUR?" Jenny asked in a worried voice. She was afraid that somehow, through some accident, they had hurt their automated friend.

"I haven't a clue," Ronald sighed. "I'm stumped. Let's check the instruction manual and see if we can find a solution to this problem."

Fortunately, an instruction manual was contained in the spare parts kit. Oddly enough, the manual was a strange silvery tablet, not a printed booklet. By just *thinking* of a question, Ronald or Jenny could cause the manual to print its answer on a silvery display screen.

RUR is frozen in his tracks, Ronald thought, concentrating on the tablet. It became warm in his hands as it received his thought-waves.

HOW WAS THE ROBOT PROGRAMMED? asked the tablet, the words forming on its screen.

Through voice command, Ronald replied. *Jenny and I both asked RUR to clean our rooms.*

BOTH AT THE SAME TIME? asked the tablet.

Yes.

THEN THAT IS THE PROBLEM. I WILL EXPLAIN: THE UNIVERSAL ROBOT HAS A LIMITED AMOUNT OF MEMORY AND BRAIN-POWER TO DEVOTE TO YOUR INSTRUCTIONS. WHEN ASKED TO DO TWO THINGS AT ONE TIME, THE ROBOT'S CIRCUITRY BECOMES OVERLOADED AND THE ROBOT IS UNABLE TO ACT BECAUSE IT CANNOT HANDLE BOTH REQUESTS . . . AND IT HAS NO INSTRUCTIONS THAT TELL IT WHICH PROGRAM TO CARRY OUT FIRST.

THERE ARE THREE SOLUTIONS TO THIS PROBLEM. DO YOU WANT ME TO LIST THEM?

Let's see the first one.

SOLUTION NUMBER ONE IS TO ELIMINATE THE CONFLICT WITHIN THE ROBOT BY REMOVING ONE OF THE COMMANDS.

"But I want my room cleaned," protested Jenny.

"So do I," said Ronald. *What's the second solution?* he thought.

SOLUTION NUMBER TWO IS TO ADD SPECIAL CIRCUITS TO THE ROBOT'S ELECTRONIC BRAIN TO ALLOW *IT* TO DECIDE WHICH COMMAND TAKES PRIORITY.

"That's out of the question," said Ronald. "I'm no robot mechanic." He turned his attention back to the tablet. *And the last solution?*

SOLUTION NUMBER THREE IS TO WRITE A "PRIORITY PROGRAM" THAT LETS THE ROBOT KNOW WHICH PROGRAMS IT SHOULD HANDLE FIRST. BY OUTLINING CLEAR-CUT PRIORITIES FOR THE ROBOT, YOU ELIMINATE THE CONFLICT AND THE PROBLEMS IT CREATES.

"That sounds reasonable," said Ronald. *Thanks*!

DON'T MENTION IT!

"We could tell RUR to do my chores first since I'm the one who found him," said Ronald.

"Ronald!"

"But since you've been so helpful in getting old RUR running, we'll let your programs run first, Jen."

"Thanks, Ronny. Big brothers aren't always jerks, I guess."

"You're welcome. I think." He spoke to RUR then. "This is an instruction. RUR, you will always carry out Jenny's programs first. Then mine. You will not carry out my programs until you have done all of Jenny's work. Is that clear?"

RUR immediately began to move again. Without hesitation, the robot marched to Jenny's room to begin his chores.

"The instruction manual gives pretty good advice!" Ronald decided. And it did indeed. RUR performed all his tasks in the order Ronald had specified. Although RUR's face was made of unmoving metal, Ronald could have sworn that his expression was one of relief and contentment.

They could now instruct RUR by voice. But it was still easier to write longer programs on paper. Unfortunately, they had run out of the programming sheets. And most corner stationery stores don't carry supplies for robots . . .

What were they to do?

Ronald decided to try ordinary notebook paper—the kind with blue rules, five holes and a red line down the left margin. He wrote a simple program on the paper and fed it to RUR.

It didn't work.

Next he tried typing paper. That didn't work either.

Then he used his father's office stationery. Still nothing.

"So much for programming. So much for a robot," he said dejectedly. "Without the brown instruction paper, we can't write any more programs for RUR. We'll have to be content with the programs we already stored in his brain."

"Don't give up so easily," Jenny scolded him. "I bought something that might help." She took a package out of a bag she was carrying. It was a package of colored construction paper.

"Construction paper?" Ronald asked, bewildered.

"When I was in the stationery store, I saw this on the shelf, and then it hit me," Jenny began. "Maybe there's nothing magical about RUR's programming sheets. Maybe there's nothing special about them at all except for the fact that they're *brown*." She flipped through the construction paper until she found a brown sheet. "Here. Try this."

Ronald took the paper. He quickly wrote a short program for producing the multiplication table. He fed the page into the robot's mouth slot. Quick as a wink, RUR produced a sheet covered with the rows and columns of the multiplication table!

"It works!" exclaimed Jenny. "Let's buy a pack of brown construction paper and put RUR back in business!"

Ronald frowned. "It seems strange that RUR understands programs on brown paper but not on white paper or lined notebook paper," he said.

"It's no stranger than some people understanding only English and others speaking Spanish or Italian," Jenny replied.

At Ronald and Jenny Smith's house, Friday night is a fun night.

Both Mr. and Mrs. Smith work at full-time jobs. Mrs. Smith is an editor in the publications department of a large manufacturing plant. It's her job to help different departments research, write and publish reports, instruction manuals and other documents.

Mr. Smith is a foreman in one of the shops at the same plant. He supervises the work of fifty machinists, technicians and laborers. Both Mr. and Mrs. Smith are active in the church, too. As a result, they're quite busy and not often home—convenient when you're hiding a robot in your room!

On Fridays, however, the whole family gets together and eats out in a restaurant. Usually they go to a hamburger place or pizza parlor, which Jenny loves, or a Chinese restaurant, where Ronald indulges in won ton soup, egg roll and sweet-and-sour pork.

But tonight it looked like they'd never get out of the house. When Mom came home, she said, "Sorry, kids, but I'm afraid I'll have to work through the weekend to have this report"—she

tapped her bulging briefcase—"ready for the print shop on Monday morning."

"That's not fair, Mom. They shouldn't make you work on the weekend."

Their mother smiled. "To be honest, it's partly my fault. On the way home, a man jostled me on the train. I didn't have a firm grip on my briefcase, and the report—all one thousand and six pages of it—went tumbling out all over the platform. I'm afraid I'll have to spend the evening putting the pages in order again."

Just then, Dad walked in. He explained that the church council had asked him to help with the charity drive. It meant he'd have to spend the evening phoning the sixty-eight church members to ask for contributions for a charity auction. He couldn't make the calls on Saturday, since he worked that shift. And Sunday, of course, was football day.

Ronald and Jenny exchanged knowing glances. They knew they could still get to eat out and help Mom and Dad do their extra work at the same time—with a little help from a friend.

"Here are the pages of Mom's report," said Ronald to RUR as he dumped several stacks of typed sheets on the bed. "Do us a favor, RUR. Put them in order so we can go out for some spare ribs and egg roll."

"*Pizza*," Jenny said. "Not egg roll."

"PUT THEM IN ORDER?" RUR's metallic voice chimed in.

"You know, sort them. In order. One, two, three, four . . ."

"SORT. DOES NOT COMPUTE. DOES NOT COMPUTE."

"Okay," said Ronald. "Whoever made RUR didn't teach him to count. Which means we're going to have to tell him how."

"And how do we do that?" asked Jenny.

"Let's find out," said Ronald. He flipped through the stack, pulled out three pages, and laid them down on the bed, like so:

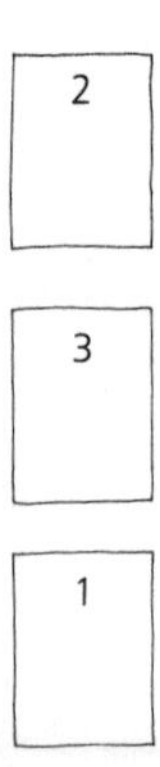

"Here are three pages from the report. They're not in order. How would you sort them?" Ronald asked Jenny.

"That's simple," she answered. "Just put the bottom one on top and they'll be in the right order." And that's what she did:

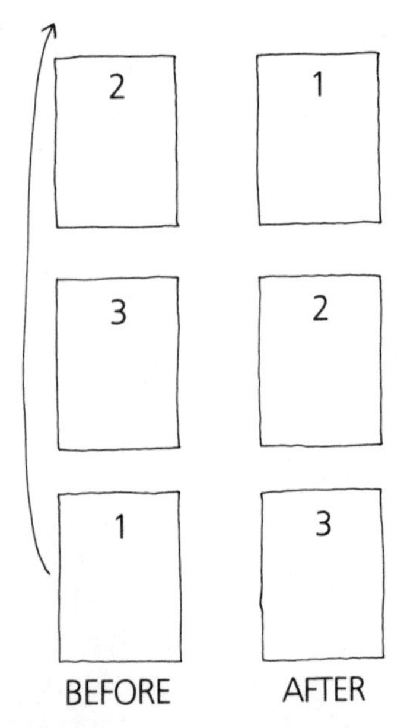

"Simple, yes. But it doesn't help RUR. He can't just look at the stack and figure out the solution like you can—that would make him as smart as a person. And he's not. He's just a machine that follows instructions—a series of numbered steps."

Ronald continued. "How would you translate your solution into robot language? With a statement that said, 'PUT THE BOTTOM ONE ON TOP'? What if the bottom page wasn't page one? What then?"

"All right, Mr. Whiz Kid. What do you suggest?"

Ronald stared at the sheets of paper. He talked as he thought out the answer. "We want to put the pages of Mom's report in order. That means the first page should have the smallest page number—page one. The page under that should have the second smallest page number—page two. And it continues in sequence until we get to the very last page, the page with the highest page number—page one thousand and six. Let's do this with the three pages here." He shuffled the pages of the report.

"First, go down the list, from top to bottom. What page has the smallest page number?"

Jenny pointed to the bottom page. "Here," she said, "page one."

Jenny finds the page with the lowest page number—page one.

"Now exchange this page with the first page," said Ronald. Jenny made the switch.

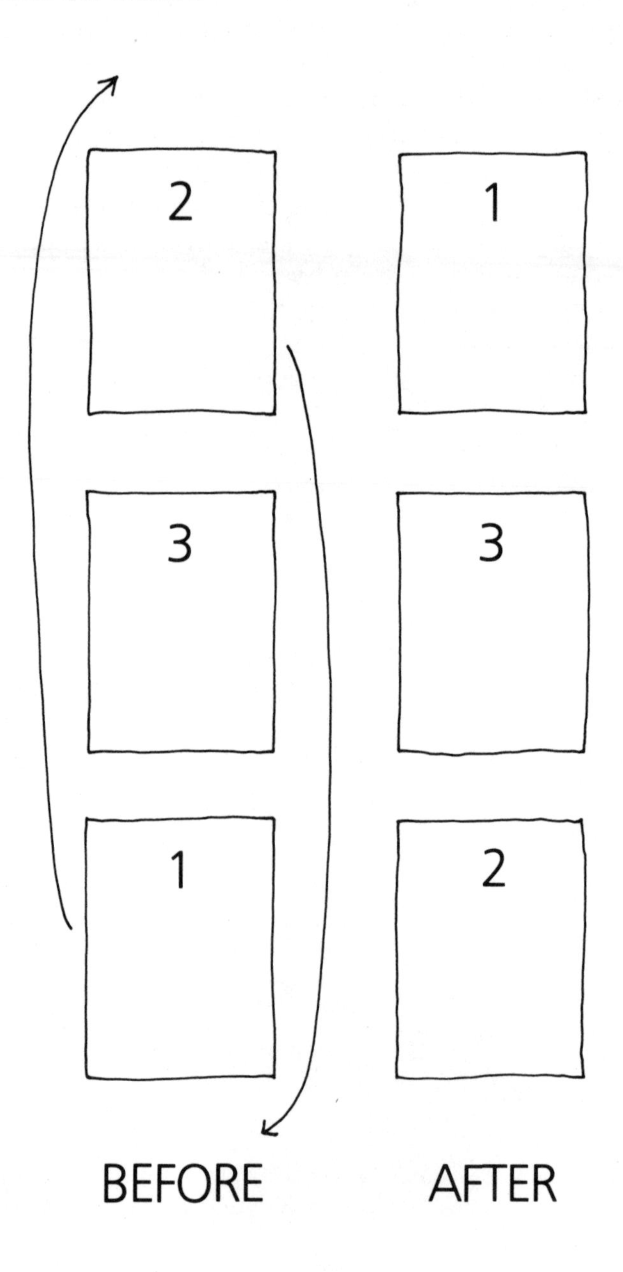

"And that'll do it."

"That's it?" asked Jenny in amazement.

"Sure. You just repeat that step going down the list until all the pages are sorted. For example, in this pile, we know that the first page is the smallest. So, starting with the second page, we go down the list. When we find the *second* smallest page number, we exchange this page with the second page in the stack."

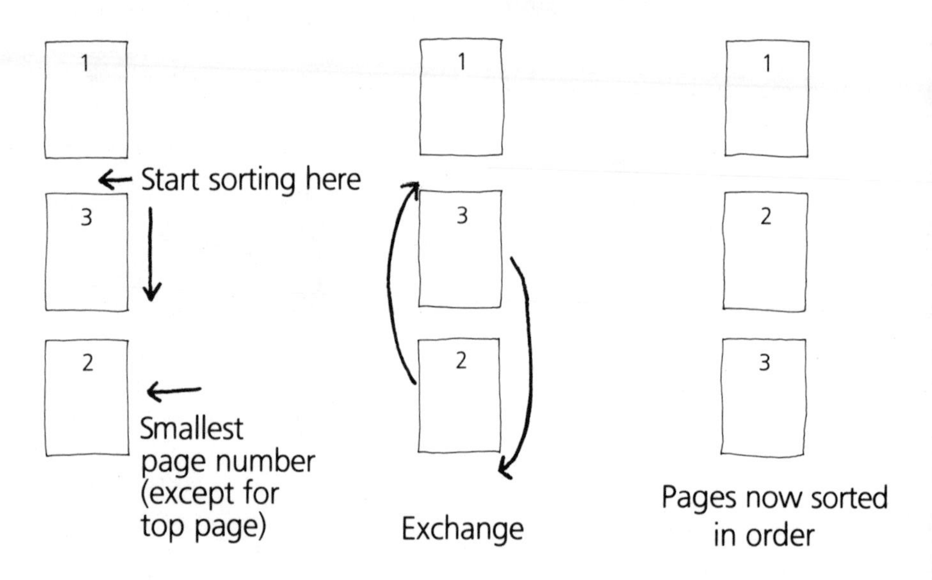

Ronald put the steps into the form of a simple program:

1 GO THROUGH THE STACK OF PAGES
2 FIND THE PAGE WITH THE LOWEST PAGE NUMBER
3 EXCHANGE THIS PAGE WITH THE TOP PAGE IN THE STACK
4 TAKE THIS TOP PAGE AND PUT IT INTO A NEW STACK LABELED "SORTED PAGES"
5 IF ALL THE PAGES ARE IN THE SORTED STACK, THEN GO TO 7
6 GO TO 1
7 STOP

Once RUR digested the program, he sorted the whole report at high speed. Within two minutes, the document was in the proper order.

Job #1 was completed. Now, if only they could figure out how to use RUR to make Dad's phone calls, they could go out to eat.

Mr. Smith was in the bathroom when Ronald took the list of church numbers he was supposed to call. Ronald didn't like to steal. But he didn't think his father would approve of handling church business with a robot.

"This is a piece of cake," Ronald told Jenny. "Here's the list of names and phone numbers, and here's the program I wrote to instruct RUR to make the calls."

Jenny looked at the program. Here's what it said:

```
1  DIAL THE NUMBER
2  WHEN THE PERSON ANSWERS, SAY "HELLO" AND
   HAVE THE CONVERSATION
3  SAY "GOOD-BYE"
4  HANG UP THE PHONE
5  IF YOU'VE CALLED ALL THE NUMBERS ON THE
   LIST, THEN GO TO 7
6  GO TO 1
7  STOP
```

Jenny shook her head. "Tsk, tsk, Mr. Computer Genius. Did you write this off the top of your head?"

"Sure," said Ronald proudly. "I've become so good at programming, I don't need to draw a diagram to help me anymore. With an easy program like this, I can get it right using plain old common sense."

"Think again," said Jenny. "I see at least two problems with the instructions you've written."

"You're nuts," said Ronald. "A *baby* could follow these instructions. You dial the number, let the phone ring, and when the person at the other end answers, you talk. That's all there is to it!"

Jenny smiled. "But what if no one answers? And what if you get a busy signal?"

Jenny was right. Ronald hadn't thought of those possibilities, and he'd have to rewrite his program. But this time he started with a diagram to see whether his solution to the problem made sense:

Program For Making a Telephone Call

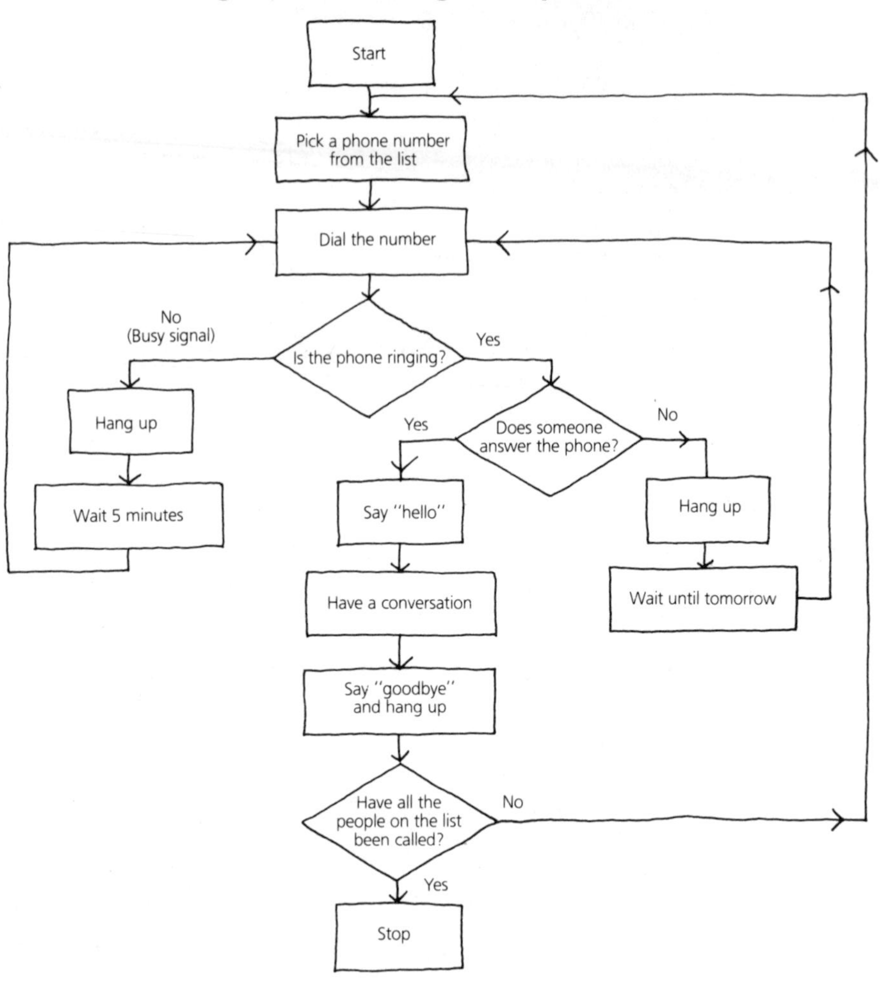

"I hate to admit it," said Ronald, "but you're right. The program does have a few 'bugs' in it . . . and I've thought of some more."

"Such as?"

"Such as: How will RUR know how many times to let the phone ring before he decides to hang up and try someone else?"

"I let it ring six times," replied Jenny.

"And I let it ring ten. But that's not the point. The point is the program has to *tell* RUR how many times the phone should ring before he hangs up—whether it's six or ten or a hundred."

Ronald and Jenny worked on the program together. They added instructions to tell RUR to hang up after eight rings. And, after a few trial runs, they got the program to work smoothly.

Mr. and Mrs. Smith were pleased—if also a bit surprised—to discover that Ronald and Jenny had taken care of Mrs. Smith's report and Mr. Smith's phone calls . . . although they weren't quite sure how Ronald and Jenny did both jobs so quickly. But in the end, everybody was quite happy that night. Except Ronald. Because they ended up going to Jenny's favorite place, Steve's Pizzeria.

And Steve's doesn't serve egg rolls. . . .

The following Thursday, Jenny was faced with an upcoming math test. Math had always been her weakest subject; she especially had trouble doing square roots, multiplication, and other simple arithmetic. And she'd really gotten rusty at it since RUR started doing her math problems for her.

What she needed was a lot of extra study time. Since she had become fairly adept at writing instructions for the robot, she decided to write a program that would let RUR become her personal math tutor.

To begin, Jenny wanted RUR to test her in multiplication.

"The idea is simple enough," she explained to RUR as she wrote the tutoring program. "I'll give you two numbers. You ask me to multiply them. I'll do it and give you the answer.

"Since you never make a mistake in math," Jenny continued, "you'll be able to tell me whether I'm right or wrong. If I'm wrong, I'll keep trying till I get it right. And when I get it right, I can either go on to another problem or end the tutoring session."

"SOUNDS SENSIBLE TO ME," RUR replied. "WHEN DO WE BEGIN?" Recently he had taken to chatting a bit with Ronald and Jenny. Maybe being around humans had caused him to pick up some human habits. Jenny had never admitted it to Ronald, but when they'd first brought RUR home, she had been afraid of him. Now she felt a fondness for the big, amiable machine. She even considered him a friend.

"We begin as soon as you eat this," said Jenny, feeding him a piece of brown paper with a program written on it.

"YUM, YUM," said RUR as he accepted the paper. Jenny had programmed him to say "YUM, YUM" whenever he "ate" a programming sheet. Ronald thought this was idiotic, but as yet had not figured out how to erase the program, much to Jenny's delight.

The logic of Jenny's self-teaching program was simple enough:

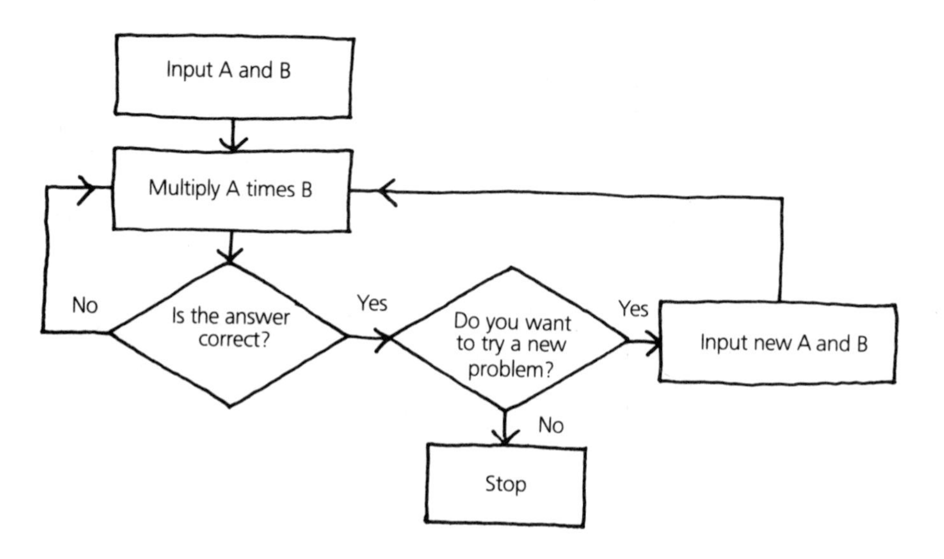

But the program itself was different from RUR's other programs. In those programs—instructions for dusting, vacuuming, and other solitary tasks—RUR would work on his own once the program was fed into his electronic brain. In the teaching program, Jenny would have a conversation with RUR! The program would instruct RUR to ask questions, and his actions would be guided by her answers.

Here is a look at her tutoring program.

```
 1  SAY: "PLEASE PICK TWO NUMBERS, JENNY"
 2  INPUT A
 3  INPUT B
 4  SAY: "WHAT IS" A "TIMES" B "?"
 5  INPUT C (JENNY'S ANSWER)
 6  LET R=A×B
 7  IF C=R, THEN GO TO 10
 8  SAY: "WRONG ANSWER, TRY AGAIN."
 9  GO TO 4
10  SAY: "THAT'S RIGHT. CONGRATULATIONS!"
11  SAY: "DO YOU WANT TO TRY ANOTHER PROBLEM?"
12  IF JENNY SAYS "YES," THEN GO TO 1
13  STOP
```

RUR began the program: "PLEASE PICK TWO NUMBERS, JENNY."

"132 and 19."

"WHAT IS 132 TIMES 19?"

She made the calculation on a piece of scratch paper.

"2498?"

"WRONG ANSWER. TRY AGAIN. WHAT IS 132 TIMES 19?"

"Whoops, shouldn't rush these things. Let's see: Nine times two is eighteen, carry the one . . . that's what I forgot to do, carry the one . . . there . . . the answer is 2508. Right?"

"THAT'S RIGHT. CONGRATULATIONS. DO YOU WANT TO TRY ANOTHER PROBLEM?"

Multiplication can be boring. But with RUR's help, it was fun to try different problems. As a result, Jenny did a lot more studying and got a B+ on the math test.

"Thanks," she told RUR when she showed him her grade. "You make learning fun, and I'm going to write programs so you can help me study other subjects in addition to math."

And although RUR was not programmed to feel happiness, Jenny was sure he was pleased to be her teacher and her friend.

To reward herself for getting a B+ in math, Jenny went shopping with her best friend Sue. Ronald said he was going to spend the day cleaning out his aquarium.

Jenny was glad to be out of the house, because otherwise Ronald would be asking for her help. She *hated* cleaning the fish tank. Her brother wasn't satisfied with a goldfish bowl or a small tank of guppies like everyone else. No. His tank was nearly four feet long and held fifty-five gallons of water. It was filled with red oscars—big, nasty fish that liked to eat little fish. Often Ronald would buy guppies or goldfish and feed them to his oscars. "Sick," she told him, "very sick."

When she got home, she checked on Ronald's progress.

He was hot, sweaty, tired, and smelled like fish. Just emptying the tank had taken him an hour—it was too big and bulky to lift, so he had to drain the water with a pail, one pailful at a time.

Ronald had already emptied the tank, scrubbed it clean, washed the gravel and changed the filter. He was about to start the toughest part of the job—filling the fish tank up with water again. He was too pooped to think about how RUR might help. But Jenny wasn't. She sat down at Ronald's desk and did some figuring with pencil and paper. Then she said, "Don't lug pails of water . . . ask RUR to do it for you."

"Write a program to fill up the fish tank?" Ronald asked. "That's a pretty smart idea. I'll do it right away, so RUR can finish the job before Mom and Dad get home."

"No need," said Jenny, handing him a page of instruction paper. "I've already done it for you."
Here's the program Jenny wrote:

1 GET A PAIL
2 GO TO THE SINK AND TURN ON THE TAP
3 FILL THE PAIL WITH WATER
4 SHUT THE FAUCET
5 WALK OVER TO THE FISH TANK
6 DUMP THE WATER INTO THE TANK
7 GO TO STEP 2
8 STOP

"Looks okay," said Ronald. "Let's try it."
Ronald took the program and fed it to RUR. The robot sprang up, seized the pail and marched straight to the bathroom sink. They heard water running. They watched as RUR carried the pail across the room and emptied it gently into the fish tank. Then, just like clockwork, the robot did an about-face and marched back to the bathroom.
Satisfied that the program was a success, Ronald and Jenny left the uncomplaining electronic servant to his boring task while they set up a game of Monopoly in the den downstairs.
Ronald was a cautious player, always counting his money. Jenny, on the other hand, bought every piece of property in sight, whether she had a chance to get a monopoly or not. Both were so intent on winning, they didn't hear the constant clumping of heavy robot feet above their heads.
Jenny was adding a hotel to Marvin Gardens when she noticed it was wet. "There's a river in Marvin Gardens," she said, pointing to a spot of water on the board.
"Very funny," said Ronald angrily. He wasn't paying attention because he was afraid that Jenny had enough hotels to beat him. He thought she was gloating about the fact that she had a hotel on Marvin Gardens.

As he picked up the dice to roll, the Monopoly board became dotted with droplets of water. They were coming from the ceiling! He dropped the dice on the floor and bolted to the stairs.

Water was pouring down the stairs like a waterfall!

He raced up the stairway, two steps at a time. Jenny followed at his heels. They nearly fainted at the sight that greeted them.

There was RUR, sloshing through water almost an inch deep on the floor. He dumped pail after pail of water into a fish tank already filled to the brim. As each pail was emptied into the tank, it sent water spilling over the sides and onto the floor. But RUR never noticed! He continued on his merry way, fetching pails of water, regardless of the fact that the tank must have been filled over half an hour ago.

"STOP!" screamed Ronald. RUR stopped in his tracks.

And then they heard the sound of their parents' car pulling into the driveway.

Needless to say, Mom and Dad were furious when they saw what had happened to the house. And they got even angrier when they found out about the robot Ronald and Jenny had secretly been keeping in Ronald's room.

After the mess was cleaned up, and Dad wasn't so mad anymore, Ronald asked his parents why the robot—who'd done his work perfectly up until then—had suddenly decided to make such a mess of things.

"From what you've told us about RUR, Ron," said Dad, "he works and thinks like a computer. Computers don't mess up unless their programmers give them bad instructions or the wrong information. Let's take a look at the program you gave RUR and see what the problem was."

Dad found the problem in an instant.

"Remember the story of the sorcerer's apprentice?" Dad asked. "The sorcerer puts his apprentice in charge of the castle in his absence. The apprentice wants to work great magic, but the sorcerer doesn't allow it. Instead, the apprentice is given the dirty work, like washing the floor of the castle.

"But the apprentice is lazy. So he uses magic to make all the mops and brooms in the castle come alive and do his bidding. He makes them wash the floor by themselves. And they do—the mops sprout arms so they can carry pails of water.

"Only the apprentice isn't skilled enough to control his magical servants. They keep bringing buckets of water, and more buckets, until the castle is flooded.

"The problem with the apprentice's magic was that it didn't include a spell to tell the mops when to stop. And that's the problem with your program.

"The program tells the robot to fill up the pail over and over again. But it doesn't have a step that says, 'CHECK TO SEE IF THE FISH TANK IS FULL. IF IT IS, STOP GETTING PAILS OF WATER.' Without that step, RUR was doomed to repeat the cycle endlessly—until someone told him otherwise."

Ronald understood. "Does this mean we get to keep RUR?"

Jenny jumped in. "Can we, can we, Dad? We'll be more careful . . . we promise."

Their father smiled. "Yes, I suppose it'll be handy having a robot around the house . . . once we learn how to use him. For starters, why don't the two of you see how you might fix the water-fetching program."

"The problem with this program," Ronald said, "is that the robot has no way of knowing when to stop filling the tank with water.

"Every time he gets to Step 7, he goes back to Step 2. That's how it's written. And there's no step between 2 and 7 that lets the robot check the tank to see if it's full. But I can fix that."

Here's how Ronald fixed the program:

1 GET A PAIL
2 GO TO THE SINK AND TURN ON THE TAP
3 FILL THE PAIL WITH WATER
4 SHUT THE FAUCET

5 WALK OVER TO THE FISH TANK
6 DUMP THE WATER INTO THE TANK
6A IF THE TANK IS FULL, THEN GO TO STEP 8
7 GO TO STEP 2
8 STOP

"That should work," said Ronald, "and I'll try it out next time I clean the fish tank. Anyway, now I know that when we tell RUR to do something over and over again, we also have to tell him when to stop. Otherwise, he'll repeat the action forever . . . or at least until one of us shuts him off."

"There's only one thing that bothers me," said Jenny.

"What's that?"

"Well," she began, "a lot of our programs ask RUR to make a decision. Or figure out something all by himself. Take the fish tank program. We ask him to look at the tank. Decide whether it's full enough. And decide whether he should put in more water. Or stop working.

"I was just wondering: How does RUR make choices? He's really more machine than person. He thinks with a brain made from wires and circuits and metal. How does a robot's brain work?"

Ronald opened RUR's spare parts kit and removed the problem-viewer. "Why don't we take a look inside RUR and find out?" he suggested.

Ronald and Jenny peered through the problem-viewer into RUR's interior. To their amazement, they saw rows and rows of tiny mushrooms! On each mushroom sat a little man, a wizened old thing, with wrinkled skin and a flowing white beard. There were hundreds of identical little men, and each smoked a tiny brown pipe.

"Who are you guys?" Ronald asked.

"My boy, we're philosophers!" one of the men said indignantly, as if Ronald had insulted him. "We analyze, philosophize, rationalize. We pontificate, elucidate, prioritize and systematize. But mostly," he sighed, "we make decisions. Compare. Contrast. That sort of thing."

"Are you *really* little men?" Ronald asked.

The philosopher coughed. "No, not really. Actually, we're all circuits that make this robot go, go, go! But without us, RUR couldn't make decisions, you know."

"And how do you make decisions?"

"Logic, my dear boy, logic. Let me explain." And he jumped up and danced a little as he recited "The Eleven Verses of Fantastic Circuits."

Everything that happens,
Everything you know,
Is the result of two decisions,
A *yes* or a *no*.

Everything that happens
Can be written using math,
And the math becomes the voltage
Flowing through a circuit path.

All that one decides
Is based on simple fact,
And from facts come conclusions
That tell you how to act.

Let's say (A) you're hungry, and
(B) hungry people need to eat.
If you're hungry AND you're people,
Then it follows—(C) you need to eat.

AND is pure logic, my friends,
And, as you can see,
It means that if A AND B are true,
Then logically, so is C.

Now, to sail the waters of logic,
You need a paddle; that's an OR.
OR is different from AND,
Thus AND is different from OR.

Let's say you're at a movie,
R-rated—what does that mean?
It means that you will get in only
If you're with a parent—OR 17.

Then there is NOT, the opposite,
But the opposite of what?
If X is a nut and you're NOT-X,
Then you're obviously not a nut.

So philosophers are a simple lot,
And you need not know more
Than that all our conclusions
Come from NOT, AND, and OR.

In robot or computer,
The logic is much the same;
Conclusions are based on statements,
And each statement is given a name.

If a circuit is ''off,'' the statement is false,
If it's ''on,'' the statement is true.
Special circuits represent NOT, AND, and OR:
The rest is up to *you*.

The little man took a final leap and landed on the ground below his mushroom.

"Is it clear to you now how we do our jobs?" he asked.

"Yes!" Jenny replied. "In RUR, electronic circuits compare the facts and make conclusions like people do. Truth is represented by an electric current, and the wiring of RUR's circuits lets him make logical decisions."

"I believe you've got it!" complimented the philosopher. And right before their eyes, his form swayed and grew misty until he and all of the hundreds of other philosophers inside RUR vanished. In place of each mushroom sat an electronic circuit, no bigger than the head of a pin.

About the author:

Robert W. Bly is a freelance copywriter who lives and works in New York City. He is the author of five books including *A Dictionary of Computer Words.*

Mr. Bly holds a B.S. in engineering from the University of Rochester.